reporting for duty.

I'm lucky I'm still around to tell my story.
It might have been very different
if I hadn't had the right stuffing.

BEAR

QUICK-DRAW McPAW

FURRY EAGLE

ONE TRUE BEAR

Ted Dewan

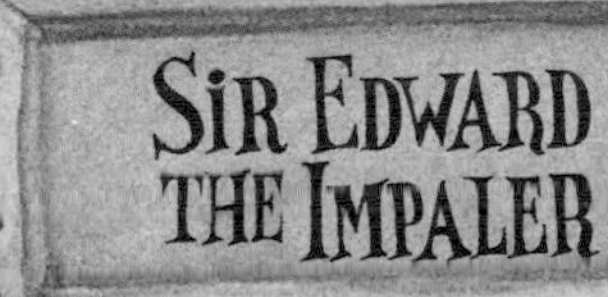

Years ago, I was a young cub serving in the Bear Force. We were having trouble with a little lad named Damian.

Bear after bear was sent away to Damian's house on an important mission: to become his One True Bear.

But even the toughest and bravest bears couldn't capture Damian's heart or imagination. He demolished them all. They just didn't have the right stuffing.

And the Bear Force was quickly running out of heroes.

One morning, our captain said to us, "I'm sure you all know about Damian. All our toughest bears have come to grief trying to become his One True Bear.

"So this time I need a bear with something truly special – I need a bear with the right stuffing. Any volunteers?"

I thought for a moment. Then I said,
"Yes, sir . . . I'm your bear."
"Darcy Brewster," said Captain,
"you are one very brave and good cub."

At sunrise the next day,
Captain said to me,
"Good luck, Darcy.
We'll watch over you."
"Thank you, sir," I said.

And I floated away from
Bear Force Headquarters,
never to return again.

When I landed at Damian's house, he picked me up and looked me in the eye.

For a moment, I thought it would all be **OK**.

But things soon got noisy.

And then things
got rough.

But I didn't cry.
I didn't fight back.
I looked him in
the eye, and said . . .

"Please . . . don't pull off my arms.

I need my arms to hug you.
If you pull off my arms, how
will I hold you at night and
keep the bad dreams away?"

So he stopped.

And I lived to see another day.

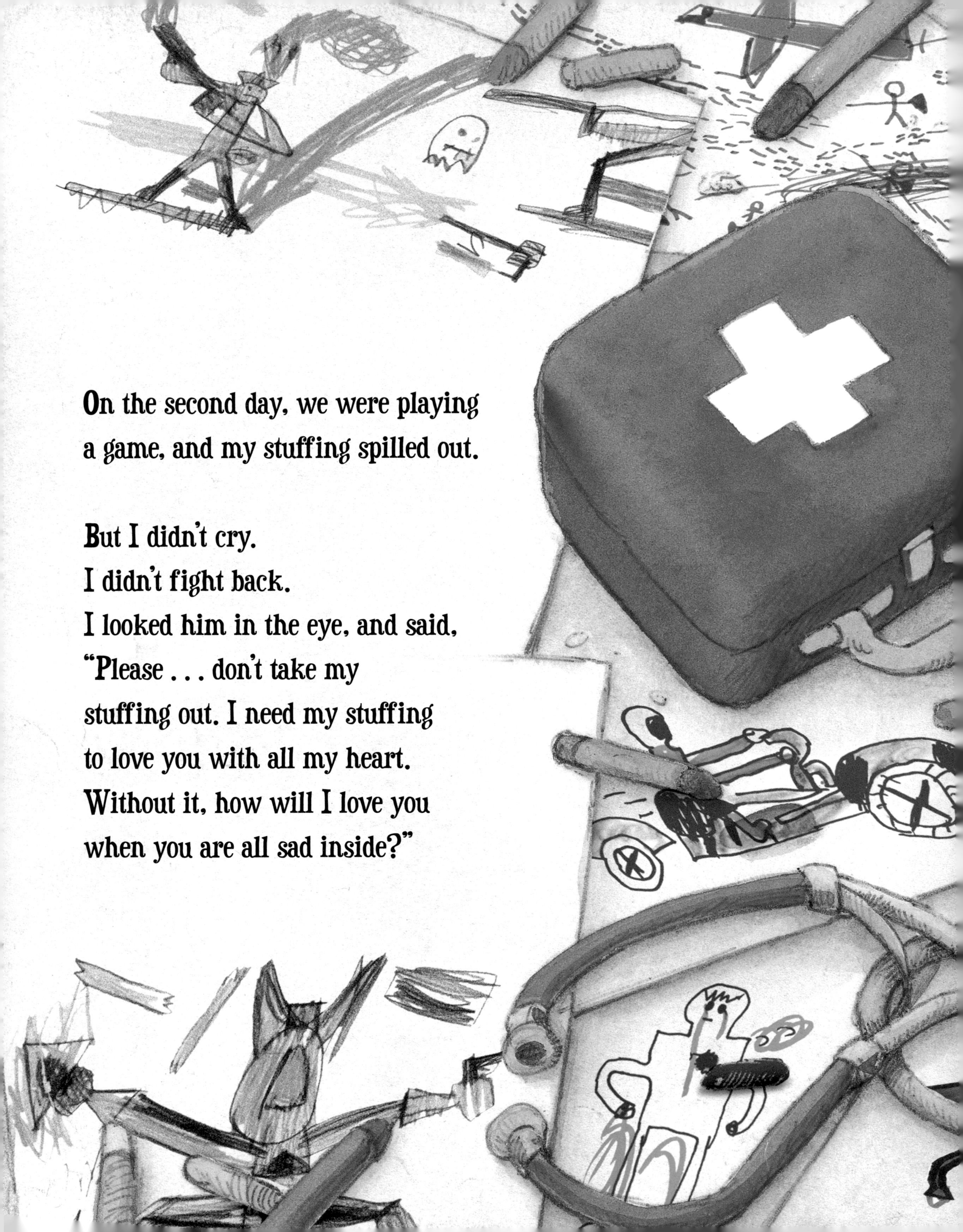

On the second day, we were playing a game, and my stuffing spilled out.

But I didn't cry.
I didn't fight back.
I looked him in the eye, and said, "Please . . . don't take my stuffing out. I need my stuffing to love you with all my heart. Without it, how will I love you when you are all sad inside?"

So he patched
up my tummy . . .

and we played
a different game . . .

And I lived to see another day.

On the third day, we went up a tree, but Damian left me there till bedtime.

So, I looked at him through his window, and said,

"Please don't leave me out here in the cold, damp night. I need my fur to comfort you. If my fur is damp and soggy, how will I comfort you when you're scared of the dark?"

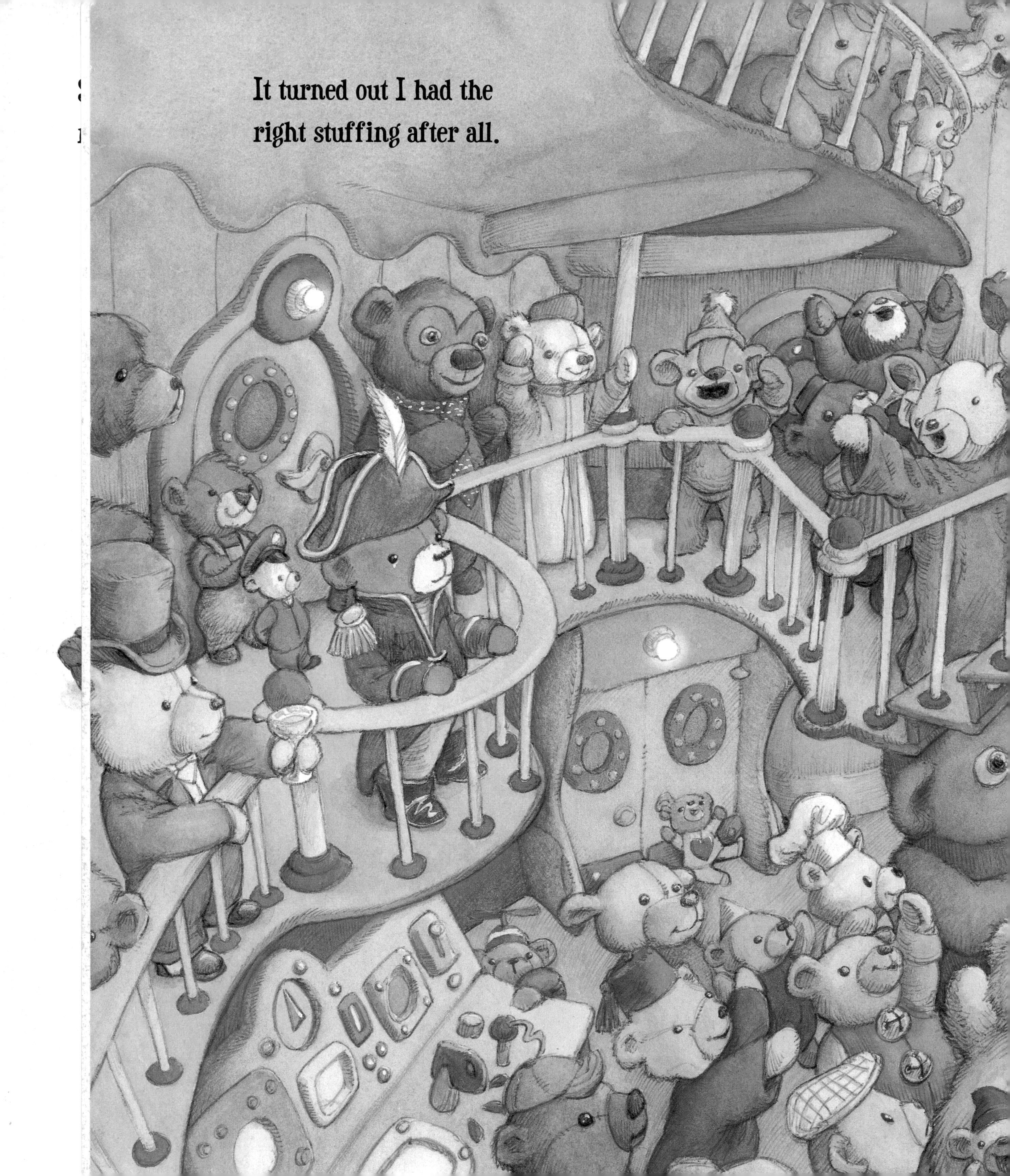

It turned out I had the
right stuffing after all.

But then one day I fell under
the bed. I stayed there all day
and all night, waiting for
Damian to find me.

I stayed there for months.
For years.
Just waiting.

Then, one stormy night,
someone came rushing into
the bedroom, pulling open
drawers and cupboards and
looking under the bed,
where finally he saw me.

He picked me up, dusted
me off, looked me in the eye,
and smiled.

It was Damian, all grown up
and dressed in a rescue uniform.
He needed me to go with him into the
storm on the toughest mission of all
and to say goodbye to him forever.

I didn't cry.

I didn't fight back.

Because after all those many, many years,
tonight I finally knew for sure . . .

. . . Damian had the
right stuffing, too.

To Pandora,
the greatest adventure

To Heather,
for sharing the dream

And to Joel,
for his courage

Special thanks to the children who contributed drawings:
Keno Burckhardt, Anastasia Bartsch, Pandora Dewan, Alfie Haddon, Greg Holyoke, Clara Osmond Kantor, Julia Monteiro, Laurence Mounce, Arthur Potts, Georgia Richardson, Jamie Selway, Leo Selway, Patrick Selway, Theo Tarrega, Desi Tomaselli, Bryony Williams, Haley Wood

ORCHARD BOOKS
338 Euston Road, London NW1 3BH
Orchard Books Australia
Level 17/207 Kent Street, Sydney, NSW 2000

ISBN 978 1 84616 715 7

First published in 2009 by Orchard Books
First published in paperback in 2010

A CIP catalogue record for this book is available from the British Library.

1 3 5 7 9 10 8 6 4 2

Printed in China

Orchard Books is a division of Hachette Children's Books, an Hachette UK company.

www. hachette.co.uk